THE VACAY

TERROR SHOCKING SECRET

THE VACAY

DEVON COMMONS

THE VACAY
TERROR SHOCKING SECRET

iUniverse books may be ordered through booksellers or by contacting:

iUniverse
1663 Liberty Drive
Bloomington, IN 47403
www.iuniverse.com
1-800-Authors (1-800-288-4677)

ISBN: 978-1-5320-4882-1 (sc)
ISBN: 978-1-5320-4883-8 (e)

Print information available on the last page.

iUniverse rev. date: 06/08/2018

THERE was a time in the early 90's where two lovely couple's. Carrie an Frank was going on a getaway trip for their 15 anniversary. The too has so much and common Carrie is a 27 years old woman with one child that frank took in as a real daughter frank Is a middle age man and he's 40 years of age both are going to visit a nice Cabin in the woods by the lake for There anniversary these Location is Hardwick, Blairstown in New Jersey August 20,1992

Fade In…

Beginning Credit

Music playing (don't stand so close to me)

EXT. Driving on a long road-day.

Caption: August 20, 1992

Smoking a cigarette bobbing Their head.

EXT. pulls over on the side of the road.

(stop music)

EXT. the side of the road-day.

> Frank gets out of the car throws his cigarette
> while he walks toward the woods to urinate.

> Carrie(smiling)
> Bae where almost there

> FRANK(chuckles)
> I know baby I really had to go.

> Carrie
> Okay so, come on let's go.

So, Frank zips his pants up and he started to walk back toward the car. Frank opens the car door to get in shuts the door behind him Frank looks at Carrie and he smiles with joy.

> Frank
> I love you Carrie. I'm glad we are together
> on this trip to have a great time.

> Carrie
> Yes, love you to baby come on let's go!

So, Carrie drives back onto the road for 3miles to their destination. Carrie turns the volume up to hear the music on the radio.
(pop music playing low)

EXT. Car driving-Day

Frank
Baby where's my pills I take for my heart? don't
want to have a heart attack out here.

Carrie
There are in the backseat and the green gym bag.

Frank
Ok.

So, Frank unbuckles his seat belt to reach under the back seat to grab his prescription out the green gym bag.

(music stop)   frank(smiling)

I really needed that but Hey, you remember we first met at the block party.

At Charles house my old high school friend I was toasted that night and young. You were a suburban girl from the other side at a block party.

Carrie

And.

Frank

And, you were just standing there looking all shy
by the couch with your friends. I walked over
after looking at you distance away by the kitchen
dining room. An I said what's your name?

With a cigarette in my left-hand beer in the right.
You replied and said Carrie with a mean look on
your face. But I understand why because I had
no professional standards greeting a woman.

Carrie(smiling)
Yea but I was checking you out, but you didn't know
because really had no eye contact with you. You
didn't even know glad you came over and said hi,
And I replied with my name which
is Carrie and yours I said.

Frank(chuckles)
Yea, we had a great time that night. After Charles
mom ended the party because a fight broke out
with Elvis. The police had to come out.

Carrie
OH, but that's in the past. It's been 15
years sense we been together we need to get
married. And you never purposed to me.

Frank
I will, I wasn't ready. But I got a surprised.

Carrie
What!

Frank
You'll see

Carrie
OH, really.

EXT. gas station/ parking lot-DAY.

so, frank and Carrie finally arrive at a gas station to get some
gas after driving a long ride behind. Frank gets out the car
shuts car door behind him walks toward the front door of
the store opens door out and didn't see store clerk behind
the counter to the right.

Int. instore-day.

Frank
Hello! Clerk.

Store clerk
Be there in a minute. I was unpacking new stock.

So, the store clerk puts the box down that he had in his right-hand. He started to walk toward the front counter.

Store clerk
How-can I help you sir?

Frank
Forty on pump 1.

Store clerk
Cash or debit?

Frank
Debit.

Store clerk
Credit, debit, down cash only.

Frank
Well I be damn, cash only. Twenty-five dollars
is all I have on me that's not enough.

Store clerk
What are you going to do? Your choice, your gas.

Frank
Okay, twenty-five on pump one fuck it.
Where almost at are destination.

Store clerk
OH, really where yawl going?

Frank
Well me and my girlfriend are both taking a
vacation and we also have an anniversary.

Store clerk
Oh okay. Wow! You two aren't married?
Because you said girl that's how I figured.

Frank
No, but it's a surprised I have for her. But
thank you for the gas have a nice day.

Store clerk(smiling)
You welcome. Have a great and safe trip You and your
girlfriend. But where is the location you are visiting.

Frank
Hardwick, by the lake.

Store clerk
Um be careful I hear a lot of people
that go visit that place get left.

Behind and never come back up the hill. Must be
something out there in that direction causes people to
die and be cure from illness like cancer, heart failure,
Don't really know what the fuck is out there.

FRANK (strange expression)
We'll, thanks sir for the info Have to
go again, thanks for the gas.

EXT. walk to gas pump-day

So, frank walks out the store toward the gas pump to
pump the gas Carrie rolls window down from the driver's
side.

Carrie
Hey! what yawl was talking about in there?

Frank
Oh, he said something about strange things be
happening at Hardwick, the cabins we are visiting
you know how people have their own opinion
about something let's just enjoy are self's okay.

Carrie
Oh really. Hurry up we almost there. Looks like
1.3miles ahead can you drive the rest of the way?

Frank
Of course, so you can sleep good tonight been a long ride.

So, Frank finish pumping the gas he started to walk around
the car to the driver's side to open the door. Frank gets in
while Carrie hops over to the passenger seat. Frank starts
the car up and starts to drive back onto the road. He looks
out his rear-view mirror and sees the store clerk looking out
the window.

Store clerk looks out window while they exit gas station.

Frank
Weirdo.

So, frank continues to drive for 1.3miles to their
destination. Frank sees a stop sign he stops. and he slowly
turns left onto a bumpy dirt road for 100ft to their
destination. Frank continues to drive ahead 100ft until
they arrived at their cabin on the right-hand side he turns
right into the front entrance of the cabins. Frank continues
to drive he sees a tree ahead frank parks the car Carrie and
Frank starts to get out the car to walk toward their cabin.

So, Frank rides up to a tree to park. He turns the car off and they started to get out the car after unbuckling their seat belts. To walk toward their cabin.

EXT.BY CABIN-DAY

Carrie
Baby, you got the keys?

Frank
Yes, hears the keys to the car and the 3rd key is to open the front door of the cabin to unload are baggage's.

Carrie unlocks the trunk grabs a bag out. a glass clock drops from the bottom of the bag because there was a hole underneath the bag Carrie looks.

Carrie
Damn! Frank

So, Frank started to walk over to help Carrie with the bag. As they gathered their stuff up two old couples appeared behind Frank.

Old man (smiling)
Hey, you youngsters need help with anything?

Frank
No, thanks for asking sir. um--yawl just
coming from the lake down there?

Old man (smiling)
Um—yes beautiful day outside must enjoy
before night fall hour from now.

Frank
I hear that. Well me and my girlfriend
is visiting for are anniversary.

Old man
OH, wonderful getting married?

Carrie
Yes, we're planning on it.

Frank(smiling)
Thanks.

Old man
Yawl, have a good one you hear. Need anything
don't be afraid to ask ok. And remember close
mouth don't get fed Worley sayings.

Frank
Ok.

Dog barking as they walk away.

INT. cabin/camera going around inside cabin.

Frank and Carrie walk into their cabin looks around Frank starts to walk toward the dining room to unpack the baggage's.

Frank
Wow! This place is nice. But where's the lights looks dingy in the kitchen and the living room.

Carrie
We'll looks good to me the kitchen lights work and living room let me go up stairs into the bedrooms.

So, Carrie goes up stairs and looks around opens bathroom door straight ahead.

She turns the lights on in the bathroom and she look around.

Carrie turns the lights off shuts the door behind her. She opens the bedroom door to her right she looks around and sees scratches on the walls and the floor. Looks like somebody tried to escape and was dragged across the floor. Right beside the scratches there were light blood so, Carrie steps back slowly out the bedroom turns around and runs down stairs.

Carrie (scared)
Frank! Frank! there's blood upstairs on the floor.

Like somebody was dragged, or murder.

Frank (frightening)
Really! you know who ever was here before us,

Really, had a bad time together maybe they had an argument with each other. I'm just guessing but, pour some water on this cloth I found in are bags.

Carrie
Yes, but that looks creepy got me wondering should we be here.

So, Carrie grabs a bucket from the side of the refrigerator. She grabs the cloth from Frank turns the faucet on by the sink to put the water inside of the bucket.

While Frank was unpacking the baggage's. Carrie turns the water off from the sink. She started to walk upstairs to clean up the blood that was on the floor.

Frank
Bae, don't worry it's going to be ok might
seems strange in here but we'll be ok.

While Carrie was cleaning up the blood. She accidentally
tips the bucket of water over the bedroom floor.

Carrie
God damn!

So, Carrie starts to clean up the water she wastes over the
bedroom floor. She squeezes the cloth into the bucket to
clean more blood up, but it seems like any of the blood
wasn't coming up. So, Carrie gets up from her kneels to go
back down stairs with the bucket of water in her hands.

Frank (smiling)
You finish already baby?

Carrie
We'll, no didn't come up I figured know soap duh.

Frank
Well baby Your right. it shouldn't be that bad.

So, Frank was finishing up unpacking their clothes.
Out their baggage's. while Carrie walks over to
him and kisses him on his chick and hugs him.

Frank
Love you baby, lets go upstairs to freshen up.

So, frank and Carrie walk upstairs into their
bedroom Carrie started to put a sheet over the bed
because there wasn't any on it and a dark cover to
lay under at night with white pillows. Frank ask
Carrie was she taking a quick shower tonight.

Frank
baby is you going to take a hot shower
to freshen up been a long day?

Carrie
Yes, pass me a towel and a cloth out your
gym bag along with the soap.

Frank reaches in his green gym bag to get Carrie a towel,
cloth and soap. Carrie starts to take off her clothes to get
ready for a shower. She grabs the towel, cloth and soap
from frank. Carrie walks out the bedroom opens the
bathroom door she turns on the water in the shower she
gets in the shower and she started to sing love songs.

Camera fades away from Carrie into outside slowly moving
across the tress wind blowing-night Fades In.

INT. CABIN-NIGHT

Frank
Hey baby. What is you singing in there?

Frank started to walk out the bedroom to go see
what Carrie was singing in the bathroom.

Frank(smiling)
Carrie, baby everything ok and there?

Carrie(smiling)
OH, yes baby shower feels so damn good.

Frank(smiling)
good let me tap that ass tonight.

Carrie(laughs)
Go away! Silly I'll be out in a minute.

So, Frank walked away from the bathroom door back
into the bedroom. He started to open the curtain
window it appears to be man walking toward the lake.

EXT. cabin/lake-night

Man outside
Hey! Where Are you? I'm hurting need you.

Need medicine wife getting on my nerves

So, Frank looks closely out the window.

Frank (shakes his head)
Weirdo.

As Frank was looking closely out the window, he sees a small guy that looks like a warlock, with a long beard and a tall hat. Suddenly Frank feels a tap on his shoulder he turns around it was Carrie.

Frank (scared)
Shit! You fucking scared me.

Carrie
What's wrong?

Frank
There was a man outside walking toward the lake talking to himself. Saying he needed help or something and I also seen a small midget standing by a tree dressed like a damn warlock.

Carrie (laughing)
Wow! now you are seeing leprechauns

Frank
Yes! no come on I'm serious but whatever.

So, frank puts out his cigarette in
the corner of the window.

Carrie
Now tell me why did you put that out
in the corner of the window?

Frank
Sorry, no ashtray.

Carrie started to sit down on the edge of the bed.
To lotion her legs, and feet to freshen up. After
Carrie was done freshening up she gets up off
the bed to turn off the lights in the bedroom.
Carrie pulls the cover back to lay down.

Carrie
Bout time we get to lay down. Now we
are going to have a great sleep.

Frank
Yes, goodnight

Carrie
Goodnight.

So, Carrie and Frank close their eyes to rest.
Suddenly they heard a loud noise coming
from the bottom of the cabins.

Women
Stop! Leave him alone.

Frank awakes.

Frank
Carrie you hear that?

Carrie
Yea I think it's coming from outside
sounds like the old women.

So, Frank and Carrie immediately jump up from their side
of the bed. And walk toward the window to see what was
going on down there. But they didn't see anybody out side
or by the lake but suddenly a light comes on down by the
cabins below.

Int. camera fade in/ cabin down below wind below-night

Ext. cabin-night

Inside cabin down below there was an old woman standing near the stairs holding a broom looking up.it appears to be a small creature with a tall hat, and gold buckles on his shoes standing at the top of the stairs holding her husband by his head.

Old women (frightening look)
Please, let my husband go! Stanley is this
who you been sneaking out with?

Creature
I want to heal him of disease I want to cure him.

Old women
What, is you talking about how?

So, the creature looks at the old man and smiles with electrical powers coming from the creature hands onto the old man body.

Old women
Please! Stop you hurting him.

The old woman starts to run upstairs where the creature was with a broom she held up in the air to attack the creature.

The creature paralyzed her whole body stopping her from attacking him. The old woman falls backwards down.

The stairs hitting her head first breaking her neck.as she rolls down the stairs blood started coming from the side of her head. The creature releases his hand from Stanley's body the old man.

He looks and said

Old man
I feel better than ever thanks.

Old man looks down below the stairs.

Old man
What have you done with my wife you little baster?

The old man slowly walks down the stairs.

Old man (crying)
…. oh baby, lord Jesus!

The old man finally reaches the bottom of the stairs. And he sees his wife laying there dead. The old man starts to touch her suddenly the creature appeared behind the old man he turns around the creature was standing in front of his face. the old man tries to grab the creature, but the creature grabs his chest and crushes the old man's heart from the inside.

Old man
You little baster.

The old man falls onto his wife. Suddenly the creature hears a knock at the door.

Frank
Anybody! Open the door I'm calling police.

The creature started to walk slowly away from the front door to the back by the kitchen door. While Frank was banging on the door to get in. so Frank lift his right leg up to kick in the door. Carrie runs out their cabin to see what was going on over there with Frank. So, after Frank kicks in the door he sees 2 old people laying there dead on top of each other.

Frank (scared shaking)
Hey! Somebody call the police.

EXT. cabin-night

So other people started to come outside from there cabins to hear and see what was going on out there.

INT. living room/cabin-night

So, frank sees a shadow coming from the kitchen back door.

Frank
Hey! Who's there say something got damn!
you killed those poor people didn't you?

The creature runs into the dark.

Frank
Come Back here!

Frank runs toward the kitchen back door to chase the creature. But he stops, and he sees the creature running through the woods Carrie walks through the front door and sees the 2 old people laying there dead. So, Carrie goes by the phone that was sitting near a table. She picks the phone up and dials 911 the phone rings twice a 911 operator picks up.

911 operator
911 what's your emergency?

Carrie(shaking)
Hello! Ma'am I would like to report a murder.

911 operator
What's your location ma'am?

Carrie
Blairstown, by the cabins.

911 operator
Someone is coming out.

So, Frank comes back inside the cabin he sees Carrie hanging up the phone.

Frank
You, call police?

Carrie
Yes, there on the way

Frank
Great, I seen the son of bitch!

Carrie
Who was it?

Frank
I don't know before I can get to him he
runs through the woods it Was dark.

EXT. cabins

So, frank and Carrie walk out the front door leaves door crack wind bellowing mild outside Carries hair goes up as she walks.
Frank looks to his right sees a man coming towards him.

MAN
Hey! What went down in there. You know?

Frank
Looks like murder two, they probably were arguing.

Carries sees bright lights coming from down
the hill shining toward their direction.

Man
Look! It's the cops.

Carrie
It is hey! Over here.

Carrie and the other people waves their hands back and
forth to get the cops attention. And there were 3 cop cars
coming their way plus 1 ambulance truck. The cops and the
ambulance truck arrive in front of the cabins they started
to get out their vehicle's while the medical team grabs their
medical gear and stretcher.

Police men 1
What's going on?

Woman
It's been crazy sir. there's to dead old people inside.

Frank
Come check it out officer.

So, Frank and 2cops, and the medical team goes inside the
cabin.one of the medical team started to check their pulse.

Ambulance man 1
Not breathing.

Frank
No shit.

So, the two men from the medical team starts to put the old man and the old woman inside a black body bag onto a stretcher. And rolls both outside the cabin to the ambulance truck.

Police man 2
Did, any of you see what happen in here?

Frank
…..know we heard noise from are
bedroom on are way to sleep.

Carrie
We came down to see what was going on. But about time we got down here they were dead.

But my boyfriend said he seen
someone by the kitchen door.

Frank
But, he ran into the woods I seen him.

Police man 1
Know description of the person.

Frank
It was dark just seen a shadow of him.

Police man 1
Ok, so that's all yawl know anything else?

Frank
No sir.

Carrie
I wish we had more info officer. This is crazy

Policeman 1
Ok everybody wraps it up

So, Frank started to walk out the front door of the cabin while Carrie was just standing there with a sad look. And the crime scene investigators started to take pictures of the scene.

The detective lights a cigarette while he walks out the front door.

INT. cabins-night.

> Detective
> Here's my card. If you see that son
> of a bitch give me a call.

The crime scene investigators cover the scene with crime tape. While Carrie walk out the front door of the cabin she hugs Frank and the police men stared to get. Back into their cars along with the medical team. The creature was looking at them behind a tree with yellow eyes glowing.

Camera fades out/red and blue cop lights flashing.

FADES In.

INT. Bedroom-morning

Frank opens his eyes to the bright sun light that was shining through the window Carrie turn over to frank.

> Carrie
> Good morning baby it was a weird night last night.

> Frank
> Yes, tell me about it I don't know what happen
> last night never seen anything like that.

Frank starts to get up from his side of the bed along with Carrie. He walks out the bedroom into the bathroom to brush his teeth. While Carrie walks toward the window to look out and she sees a dog barking down below by the lake while other people were swimming in the lake. she closes the curtains and turns around to walk out the bedroom where frank was.

Carrie
Baby would you like to go for a swim today.

Frank
Hell yea! let's go fresh my mine for what happen
last night never seen a dead person before
but whoever did that well be punish.

Carrie
Yup let's just enjoy are day today because
we're here for a good vacation.

So, Frank puts his swimming trunks on along with his sandals. Carrie grabs her swim wear out Frank gym bag they both started to walk out the bedroom to walk down the stairs after frank grabs a towel from the dresser.

EXT.by the lake-day.

Frank and Carrie walks toward the lake as they walk a woman approach them from a distance by the cabin where those old people were killed.

Women
Hey! You guys going for a swim on this beautiful day.

Frank

Yes, what about you?

Woman

Well, no not at all what happen last night was very curl.
Those poor older people it's something out here be aware.

Frank

Thanks, but I'm trying to clear my head I was new to that.

Woman

Yea, yawl have a good day ok.

Carrie

Bye.

So, frank an Carrie continue to walk toward the lake.

Carrie

Hey, baby I know it might be a little bit cold in there.

Frank

I no. follow me

Frank runs and jumps into the lake after he throws the towel
to Carrie.

Frank (shacking)
Cold...

So, Carrie walk toward the lake and she puts her feet in the water smiling at Frank. While he was swimming in the lake.

Frank
You scared get in bae enjoy yourself.

Carrie (smiling)
Ok when I'm ready silly.

Frank swims toward Carrie as she sits on the edge of the rock. Frank gets out the water and he kiss Carrie on her chick.

Carrie starts to give Frank the towel that was laying next to her by the rock. Frank starts to dry off.

Carrie
That was fun or what?

Frank
It was great! And wonderful

Franks gets up off the rock he started to feel chest pain for some reason.

Carrie
Baby what's wrong? oh know where your pills?

Frank
In the house Go get them.

Little boy
You ok Mr.?

Frank
I'm fine oh my god Carrie.

Carrie started to run toward the cabin to grab Frank prescription. While the little boy was keeping Frank company.

So, Carrie opens the front door of the cabin. Runs upstairs to grab Frank pills out the Chester drawer. She moves the cloths around to grab the pill bottle Carrie close the drawer and she started to run back down stairs to the kitchen to get a bottle of water out the refrigerator. Carrie grabs the bottle of water and she runs back out the door to go back down by the lake.

Carrie
OK, move out the way here baby take this. So, Frank swallows two pills along with the water.

Frank

Oh my god please help me.

The pain from Frank chest started to
calm down to a normal level.

Frank

I must lay down for a while.

Frank gets up from the grass while Carrie whips the grass off his back.

EXT. cabin lake-day.

Little boy

Hope you feel better Mr.

So, Carrie puts her arm around Frank waste and they both walked back to their cabin, so Frank could lay down.

Carrie

Its ok baby. wait here while I take a quick shower.

Carrie walked out the bedroom into the bathroom to take a shower. Suddenly Frank hears a loud noise coming from down stairs in the kitchen. Frank gets up from the bed to go see what was going on down stairs. He started to walk out the bedroom slowly walk down the stairs into the kitchen he sees silverware and knives over the kitchen floor.

> Frank
> Hello! is somebody there? If there is. you
> have an ass whooping coming.

Frank continues to walk out the bedroom to walk down stairs. Frank gets to the bottom of the stairs he looks around and he sees all the cabinets were open in the kitchen with silverware all over the kitchen floor.

> Frank
> Who's here?

Frank grabs a knife off the floor walks slowly across kitchen floor.

> Frank
> Come out I know you in hear.

Frank looks around the corner by the dining room sees a shadow runs by.

> Frank
> Hey... hey!

Frank walks toward the shadow but it disappears as he was walking toward the shadow. Suddenly Frank feels a body sense behind him Frank turns around the creature appeared in front of his face.

Frank
Screams!!!

Frank drops his knife on the floor and falls backwards on the dinning room floor. Carrie heard a loud noise upstairs in the shower, so she started to turn the water off in the shower. Carrie gets out the shower grabs the towel that was on the sink she dry's off quickly and she wraps the towel around her. Carrie walks out the bathroom and looks in the bedroom she didn't see Frank, so she slowly walk by the stairway.

Carrie
Baby are you there?

Carrie walks down the stairs and she sees the cabinets open with silverware all over the kitchen floor. she looks around the kitchen corner it appeared to be Frank laying there shacking.

Carrie
Oh! Baby what happen?

So, Carrie grabs frank off the dining room floor and she started to walk him toward the stairway to lay him down. Frank starts to wake up.

> Carrie
> What happen who was here why is
> everything is everywhere?

Frank looks at Carrie with a terrifying look.

> Frank
> It's here.

> Carrie
> What?

> Frank
> It's a monster I figured. and it was ugly
> as hell I think we found are killer.

> Carrie
> What is going on? We see too dead
> people now your saying he's here.

> Frank
> This is crazy!

Frank gets up from the floor and walks up stairs.

> Carrie
> Can you please pass me a cigarette in the first drawer?

Frank reaches in the drawer to grab Carrie a cigarette out the Newport box and he throws 1 down stairs to Carrie.

Frank
Heads up!

Carrie catches the cigarette along with the lighter that Frank threw down stairs.

Carrie
(smoking)
I'm going outside for a minute okay.

Frank
Sure. I'm still thinking about what was that I have to lay down body feels tierd.

So, Frank walks into the bedroom lays down on the bed Carrie tries to pick up the silverware that was on the kitchen floor. But she opens the door instead to go outside she looks around outside while she lights a cigarette. and she started to walk toward the lake where she seen a woman standing with her arms in the air.

Carrie
Hi, ma'am you ok?

Old woman
OH, yes darling praying to my father
above giving him the glory.

Carrie
Good I'm a Christian.

Old woman turns around at Carrie and smile.

Old woman
So, you are? never seen you around

Carrie
Of course, you haven't me and my boyfriend
is on a get away for are 15th anniversary

Old woman
Good. But why here?

Carrie
Why you say that?

Old woman
It's been too much going on lately those poor people died
I was friends with the wife husband
was sick but every time I seen
Him he always seems to be fine.

Carrie
My boyfriend has a heart problem.

Old woman
Have he been treated?

Carrie
Oh, yea he's been taking pills to come it down.

Old woman
…good it's something out here that has a cure for
wellness have you seen it yet. If it fears it kills

Carrie (serious look)
Somebody ware in are house today Destroyed
the kitchen scared my boyfriend while I was
in the shower. And I think it was the man
that killed those old people that night.

Old woman
If it made a way to you. You're in danger.

Carrie
What did it come from?

Old woman
We don't know…. I been in this area for 25
years never seen anything like this.

Carrie

Wow the detective said too call if we see this man
my Boyfriend said he did it's a man isn't it?

Old woman

…. we don't know never seen anybody been
cured from a illness without seeing a doctor.

Carrie

Yea, true

Old woman

So, you be careful out here you and your
man if you see it ask what's its purpose.

Carrie

Ok.

So, Carrie hugs the old woman and she turns around to
walk back toward her cabin. Carrie opens the front door of
the cabin and she yells frank name.

INT. cabin-day

Carrie

Frank! Baby

Carrie walks upstairs while calling franks name she opens bedroom door walk toward him to the right shakes him on his shoulder.

Carrie
You ok?

Frank
(Yawning)

Carrie
Get up baby

Frank whips both of his eyes look at Carrie.

Carrie
Yes baby, you ok now? I talked to a woman down by the lake she knows a little bit about the man that killed those old people that night. But she doesn't even know if it's a man or creature.

Frank
What you mean creature? I was so scared I didn't really know what it was.

Carrie
If, we see this thing tonight or sometimes let's see what's his purpose.

Frank gets up out of the bed walk toward the bathroom to urine fleshes toilet.

Turns sink faucet on to wash his hand and face.

Frank
Hey! Grab a towel.

Carrie grabs a towel to give to Frank, so he could dry his hands and face. Frank walks back into the bedroom to look out the window.

Frank
Don't nobody be out during the day.

Carrie
Yes, down by the lake.

Frank
Well I'm stepping outside for a minute.

Carrie
Do you have your pills just in case?

Frank
Yes.

So, Frank starts to take off his swimming trunks and sandals. To put on some pants and a shirt to go outside. Frank kisses Carrie on the chick after putting on his cloths on to go down stairs to go outside for a minute while Carrie cleans the kitchen.

Camera fade out by the woods.

FADE IN

Franks starts to walk through the woods behind a cabin. he reaches in his pocket to grab a cigarette with a lighter to smoke as he walks through the woods. Suddenly Frank sees somebody ahead dancing around a tree.

Frank
Who's there?!

Frank slowly throws his cigarette while looking ahead at the creature dancing toward him.

Frank
What do you want ass hole?

Creature (echo's)
I want to help you frank.

Frank
What?

Frank continue to walk the creature had disappeared frank looks

Frank (think out loud)
Where did he go?

Frank looks to his right the creature jumps in front of him. Frank falls to the ground.

Frank
What do you want with me?

Creature
I want to help you get better. Don't you want better frank?

Frank
How is that?

Creature
Just give me your hand

Frank started to put his hand toward the creature.

Frank
Know! Get away.

Frank starts to run out the woods
while the creature laughs

Creature
You can't run I'll be back you want be disappointed.

Frank trips over a log while he was running through the woods. Suddenly Frank chest started to hurt he squeezes his chest with his right hand.

Frank
Fuck! Help me somebody

Carrie finally cleans the kitchen up along with the silverware that was on the kitchen floor. She started to walk upstairs to the bedroom Carrie looks out the window and she sees two guys walking holding Frank by his arms.

So Carrie started to go back out the bedroom she runs down stairs to the front door. to see what was going on with Frank.

Carrie
Hey baby, did you have a small heart attack again.

Carrie tries to grab Frank from the two guys.

Guy
Move back lady we seen him lien there
bought to die let us take him inside ok stand
back where's your cabin? go open it.

So, Carrie runs toward the cabin to open the door for the two guys.

Guy 2
Where's your room? get some cold water

They started to walk frank up the stairway to his room.

Carrie
Lay him down on the left side of the bed.

So, the two guys lay Frank down on the bed. And Carrie started to pour water on his face with a bottle of water that she had on the side of the bed.

Carrie
Wake up frank it's me honey

Frank started to open his eyes slowly.

Guy (smiling)
Hey! He's awake.

Frank looks around the room and he sees two guys standing over him.

Guy
You were almost out of here buddy

Carrie
Thanks, to god and these guys.

Frank
Where's my pills?

Carrie
Right, here.

Carrie grabs frank pills take 1 out gives it to frank with the water bottle she had poured on him.

Frank
Thanks.

Frank swallow the pill down while the two guys walks out the bedroom.

Guy 2
You take it easy Frank. Don't leave him out there
if you know he has a bad heart condition.

Carrie
I know…did you see something out their Frank?

Frank
Yes.

Carrie
What, was it?

Frank
The creature…it spoke and said he wanted to help me.

The two guys walk out the room while Carrie talks to frank.

Carrie
This is crazy!

Frank
This thing is after us now.

Carrie
I want to go back home it's so much going on out here.

Frank
We will baby I see that mother fucker
again he will get handle.

So, Carrie started to get up from the edge of the bed and
walks down stairs frank lies there thinking to himself while
looking up to the ceiling. Carrie sits on the sofa by the
front door suddenly she hears thunder coming from outside
Carrie looks toward window by front door rain drop hits the
window it started to rain hard outside.

Carrie
Well, I be damn rain.

Carrie stretches her legs across the sofa to lie down.

EXT camera rolling through the woods raining-evening cloudy.

So, the creature appears near abandon cabin in the woods looking through the rain. The creature started to walk toward the cabins ahead as the creature walks he disappears.

INT. Bedroom-evening
Frank starts to get up from the bed and he walks toward the window.

Frank
Damn, it's raining Carrie

Carrie didn't answer frank starts to turn around to walk out the room frank walks down stairs sees Carrie lien their sleep. Hand across her chest.

Frank
Baby getting some rest.

So, the rain starts to slow down Frank grabs an umbrella out the closet by the front door. He opens the front door to go outside.

Frank looks at Carrie while he closes the door behind him. He starts to walk toward the lake while the rain was slowly coming down from the sky. Suddenly the creature appears by a tree Frank turns around and he sees the creature.

EXT. outside cabin-evening

Frank

Hey! I see you come here!! I got you now motherfucker.

Frank starts to run toward the woods where the creature was standing creature starts to run through the woods while frank chases him.

Frank

Come Back here!

Creature lead him toward the abandon cabin where he lives frank starts to slow down breathing hard bent over to catch his breath frank looks up creature disappears.

Frank

What the fuck. Where did he go?

Frank sees an old cabin ahead with busted windows. As he walks closer looks like the door was off its hinges

Frank

Hello! Where are you?

Creature stands behind a big tree ahead looking at frank while he walks up toward cabin.

Frank

Come, out! No more running you hear me.

Frank looks around didn't see creature nowhere frank walks toward cabin door push door open it was kind of dark inside.

But a little light was shining through a window the creature starts to walk slowly into the cabin behind Frank. Suddenly Frank hears foot steps behind him so, he turns around the creature was in front of his face Frank was terrified he started to reach in his pocket to grab his pills. but the creature grabs his arms Frank drops his pills on the floor while electrical powers was coming from the creature hands onto Frank body.

INT. cabin Livingroom-night

Carrie looks out the window the rain starts to stop. She opens the front door of the cabin and she yells Frank name.

Carrie

Frank! You there?

Carrie didn't get no reply she starts to walk upstairs into the bedroom didn't see frank nowhere checks bathroom frank wasn't there. She runs back down stairs.

> Carrie
> Now, where did he go.

Carrie opens the window in the bedroom to yell Frank name again.

> Carrie
> Frank!!!!

EXT. outside cabin-night

No reply she starts to walk toward the woods where she figures frank may have went.

Camera fades out by the cabin where frank and the creature where

FADE IN

So, the creature releases his hands away from frank body frank falls to the floor while the creature walks away.

> Creature
> You will feel better no, more pills you
> hear. trust me I'll take care of you.

Camera fades out

Fade in

Carrie continues to walk through the woods searching for frank.

Carrie
(yells)

Frank!!! Where are you?

Carrie continues to walk, and it was very dark ahead. know flashlight or nothing. Suddenly Carrie hears a stick break near a tree ahead. It was Frank coming from behind a tree.

Carrie
Damn! Frank is that you?

Frank
Yes.

Frank
He touched me. He had powers.

Carrie
What is it?

Carrie
I thought you was sleep for god sake.

Frank

He said he wanted to take care of me I feel better.

Carrie

What did he do to you frank?

Frank

I feel better it don't hurt no more.

Carrie

Where is your pills?

Frank

In the cabin behind us I left them.

Carrie

Why? I'm going back home because this is weird.

So, Carrie and Frank continue, to walk out the woods. Carrie started to put her arm around Frank waste.

It appeared to be a man standing near a cabin ahead looking at them while Carrie and Frank get closer to exit the woods. Carrie releases her arm from around Frank waste.

Man

You ok? Sweetie

Carrie
I'm fine what is it with you people around here?

Man
What you mean honey? Just trying to
see if you're ok you the one
Talking to yourself.

Carrie and frank continues to walk pass the man standing
by cabin near woods.

Carrie
Don't you see my boyfriend hurt here?
bout to run out of breath.

Man
What, boyfriend you been drinking?
don't see no man sweetie

Franks puts his head down while walking back toward
cabin.

Carrie
Don't you see my man here he's
walking with me oh my god….

What's wrong with you people?

Carrie opens the front door of the cabin. They both walk into the living room.

INT. inside cabin-night

> Carrie
> I'm packing up frank its weird out here
> you here what that guy said
> He didn't see you.

> Frank
> Baby, listen to me stay it's are anniversary remember.

Carrie walks upstairs while frank walk behind her.

> Frank
> Where you going baby don't leave?

> Carrie
> What? Excuse me.

> Frank
> I said don't leave.

> Carrie
> OH, I'm leaving alright.

So, Carrie starts to walk out the bedroom to go down stairs with her baggage and car keys. Frank tries to grab her.

Carrie
No, get off me!

Frank releases his hand from her shoulder.

frank
Ok leave ill just sit here all by myself I told you
I feel better I want you too stay with me.

Carrie continues to walk down stairs with her baggage hitting the stairs on the way down. Carrie reaches the bottom of the stairs she opens the front door of the cabin slams the door behind her. she opens the trunk to put the baggage in, Carrie close the trunk of the car. and she opens the driver door Carrie starts the car and drove away from the cabin. It was very dark outside she turns the wheel right to exit the cabins back onto the bumpy road Going slowly. Carrie continues to drive until she got to a stop sign ahead to turn right. Carrie slowly turns right by the stop sign She continues to drive ahead suddenly she sees a short man ahead waving his arms back and forth to get Carrie attention. She turns on her front lights brighter going 30miles per hour Carrie looks closely ahead it was the creature standing there waving his hands.

Carrie tries to run him over the creature disappears.

> Carrie
> What, the fuck.

So, Carrie looks through her rear-view mirror and she didn't see the creature nowhere. Suddenly she hears a boom! The creature appeared on top of the hood of the car. Carrie screams and she hits the gas going 50miles per hour to knock the creature off the car.

> Carrie
> (yells)
> What the fuck! Do you want?

The creature punches the windshield cracks it. Carrie started to swerve across the road left to right to knock the creature off the car.

So, the creature smiles at Carrie. And he spoke in the sound of voice as Frank.

> Creature
> Your stuck here not going know where.

The creature jumps off the hood of the car. Carrie sees a tree ahead she started to hit her breaks before running into the tree. Carrie leans forward into the airbag the horn starts to go off.

Frank walks back and forth across the bedroom thinking to himself.

Frank
What the fuck! Did I do. Carrie gone, and
I'm here alone bring her back to me.

Frank starts to go out the bedroom to walk down stairs
to go outside to yell Carrie name.

Frank
(yells)
Carrie!!!

So, Carrie lift her head up slowly from airbag horn stops
Carrie opens car door.

Unbuckles her seatbelt Carrie open the car door she falls out
the driver seat onto the pavement. She was bleeding from
her forehead and a few cuts on her face.

Frank
Where are you Carrie come back!

Frank starts to walk to the front entrance of the cabins.
Frank looks down and he sees tire marks. Carrie wakes
up slowly from the pavement and she lifts her right hand
toward her forehead where she felt pain and blood.

Carrie
Oh, my god help me look at my car.

Carrie starts to limp as she walks away from her car going the opposite direction. She drags her right led across the pavement suddenly a bright light was flashing toward Carrie. It appears to be a truck driving toward her way she starts to wave her arms back and forth to get the drivers attention The truck stops. a man opens the car door and starts to run toward Carrie.

Carrie
Please! Help me I had an accident I'm
hurting its coming for me.

Carrie looks behind her and she didn't see the creature. The man starts to help Carrie to his car while putting his arm around Carrie waste.

Truck driver Sam
Who's coming?

Carrie(crying)
That man he's trying to kill me...

Truck driver Sam
I don't see anybody. Come on let's get you home.

So, the man opens the passenger door to let Carrie in. and he started to buckle her seatbelt.

Truck driver Sam
You going to be ok.

So, the man shuts the passenger side door. He started to walk around toward the driver side to get in. to hit a U-turn to drive back the other way.

EXT. driving on dark road-NIGHT.

TRUCK DRIVER Sam
SO, WERE DO YOU LIVE?

Carrie
I'm visiting me and my boyfriend.

Truck driver Sam
Oh, wow.

Carrie
"please don't" take me back there. I love my boyfriend, but he's been acting strange and weird things been going on. and my child is over her other side of the family for the summer.

Truck driver Sam
So, you don't want to go back where your boyfriend is at?

Carrie

No, I don't he's scaring me we haven't had
any time together sense we been out here
I rec the car he's going to be mad.

EXT. on bumpy road-night

Frank appeared at the end of the street by the stop sign. Talking to himself.

Ext. Car driving

Truck driver continues to drive along the dark road Carrie starts to cry.

Carrie (crying)
I don't know what to do

Truck driver Sam
Okay let's get you cleaned up. It's
going to be okay stop crying.

Carrie whips her tears from her eyes. While Sam ask for her name.

Truck driver Sam
What's your name?

Carrie
Carrie What's yours?

Truck driver Sam
Sam.

Carrie
Nice to meet you.

Truck driver Sam
You too Carrie.

So, Sam the truck driver turns left into the drive way to park.

EXT. house driveway-night.

Truck driver(Sam)
We here.

Carrie
Where?

Truck driver(Sam)
My place come on let me help you out the car.

Sam helps Carrie out the passenger seat. He walks her to the front door of his house to unlock the door.

INT.house

So, Carrie walks inside the house she looks around. Sam grabs Carrie to guide her to the back room to lay down on the bed. He lifts her head up on his pillow, so she could sit up straight. Sam goes into the bathroom to wet a cloth, so he could wipe the blood from Carrie forehead.

> Truck driver(Sam)
> There, lie down and relax I'll take
> you back home tomorrow ok.

> Carrie (tired face)
> It's been a long day.

Sam lifts her right pant leg up to rub her legs with alcohol while he was looking into her eyes.

> Carrie
> Wait a minute. don't get to comfortable
> by rubbing my legs.

> Truck driver(Sam)
> smiling
> I'm just helping you out.

Carrie
Sure.

So, Sam the truck driver walks into the kitchen to grab a cold beer out the refrigerator. Carrie starts to get up from the side of the bed she looks around the room and she seen a box sitting near the T.V. she walks toward the T.V to grab the box Carrie opens it there were old pictures and frames in the box so, Carrie starts to grab a photo out the box. there were two guys on the photo one look like Frank.

Truck driver Sam (confused look)
What…. Are you doing looking through
my stuff? You pose to be sleeping.

Carrie
What is this? it looks like frank.

Truck driver Sam
Wait a minute let me see the picture. frank who?

Carrie
My boyfriend I was telling you about.

Truck driver Sam (strange look)
That's my dad's friend, Frank was a doctor and my dad
was a mechanic when I was little. My dad uses to work
on Frank luxury cars and Frank had a cure for Aids,

cancer patients and more. He was a very smart man he helped a lot of people and was very average living.

Carrie
Wait a minute…

Truck driver Sam
But he died along with my dad. He was killed by a group of people when he left their child to die for lack of health insurance, and no money to cover the patients. They burn him alive in those cabins you are visiting. And my dad had a bad heart not Frank.

Carrie
So, you mean to tell me my boyfriend that I been with for 15years is dead no way.

Frank driver Sam
Yes, frank died years ago I was just a little boy. The cabins your visiting nobody visit that place no more Frank is dead.

Carrie
Oh my god! Take me home.

Truck driver Sam
I told you don't nobody stay over that place its abandon okay. But if you assist going back there let's go.

Sam helps Carrie up from the floor and he started to walk out the room to grab his keys.

Truck driver Sam
Lets! Go don't have all-night told you the place is abandon.

Carrie walks beside Sam to open the front door. Sam closes the door behind them and locks it.

EXT. outside drive way-night

Sam opens the passenger door for Carrie. she fastens her seatbelt while Sam close the passenger door to go around to the driver side. Sam opens driver side door to get in Sam starts the car up and close the door and he started to back up from the drive way turns wheel to the right to drive along the road.

Carrie
This is tripping me out.

Truck driver Sam
Why it's true.

EXT.DARK ROAD-NIGHT

Sam continue to drive going 40miles per hour down the dark road head lights shining bright.

> Truck driver Sam
> Frank died long time ago

> Carrie
> What! Frank has a bad heart.

> Truck driver Sam
> No, he never did.

Sam gets to a stop sign ahead and stops.

> Truck driver Sam
> We almost there you sure?

> Carrie
> Yes, take me back.

So, Sam continues to drive a minute ahead to drop Carrie off.

INT. Bedroom

Frank starts to walk inside the cabin and he closes the door behind him. He sits down on the edge of the sofa to wait for Carrie to walk through the front door.

EXT. DRIVING-NIGHT

Sam stops truck.

> Truck driver Sam
> Here you go.

> Carrie
> Thanks Sam.

> Truck driver Sam
> No, problem be careful sweetie.

EXT. walking on dark road

So, Carrie opens passenger door gets out closes door behind her Sam drives off Carrie starts to walk down the bumpy dirt road.

Toward the cabins ahead. She looks didn't see nobody outside Carrie continues to walk to her cabin finally gets to the front door of her cabin turns door knob it seems to be unlock Carrie walk in sees frank sitting there on the sofa legs cross.

INT.livingroom/cabin-night

> Frank
> What happen didn't drive home?

> Carrie
> No

Frank
So…. how did you get here?

Carrie
Frank I rec the car that thing was
after me what is going on?

Frank
Wow.

Carrie
Can I ask you a question how old are you
really? you never had a bad heart.

Frank
Wait a minute what got into you? Let me explain.

Frank starts to get up from the sofa walks toward Carrie.

Carrie
Stay away frank you lied to me.

Carrie shows Frank the old picture
that she took from Sam house.

Frank
Where did you get that?

Carrie
All these years we been together you been walking dead.

Frank
I was going to tell you, but I loved you
didn't want you to leave me.

Carrie
Your crazy! So, what's going on with those
people that died was that true?

Frank
Yes, but that happen long time ago just wanted
you to see what really happen that was my friend I
tried to save him from his illness but his wife didn't
let me the creature is me imagine so call friend

Carrie
I'm really getting out of here frank.

Frank tries to grab Carrie, so she wouldn't leave.

Carrie
Let me go!

Frank
Quite you'll wake the dead.

Carrie releases herself from frank she starts to run toward the back-kitchen door to get away from frank.

Frank

I just wanted you to see they killed me you know.

Frank grabs Carrie by her left arm stopping her from going out the back-kitchen door.

Carrie

Let me go! Already.

Frank

Stop child your waking the dead.it wasn't my fault they burn me alive in this cabin I just tried to help.

Carrie

You a murder, killer!

Carrie grabs a broom from behind kitchen door hits frank across the face to get away from him frank stumbles backwards.

While Carrie runs out the kitchen door Frank yells her name.

Frank

Carrie!!!

EXT. Cabin-night

Carrie!!

Carrie continues to run. suddenly she sees an old woman standing near a cabin with blood on her hands.

Old woman (smiling)
Wait where are you going. It's just begun?

Carrie
What!

Carrie pushes the old woman out of her way. Carrie runs into the old woman cabin closing the door behind her. Frank walks outside and he didn't see Carrie anywhere.

Frank
Where is she?

Frank helps the old woman up from the ground.

Woman
She's in my cabin.

INT. cabin-night

Frank and the old woman opens the front door of the cabin. Carrie walks slowly toward the kitchen and she grabs a pot off the stove quietly.

Frank
I know you here baby. I'm not going to hurt
you just want you to understand.

The old woman gets close to the kitchen where Carrie was hiding.

Carrie
Stay back! away from me.

The old woman hears a sound coming from the kitchen. Carrie jumps out from behind a chair hitting the old woman with the pot over her head she falls backwards on the kitchen floor.

Frank
Baby put down the weapon nobody is going to hurt you.

Frank starts to walk toward Carrie slowly.

Carrie
Don't come any closer frank your insane!

Frank continues to walk toward Carrie he tries to grab her. Carrie swings the pot hitting Frank on his hands the old woman trips Carrie off her feet Carrie falls on her back. Onto the kitchen floor. Frank grabs the pot from Carrie hands and he started to grab her pants leg.

Started to drag her out the kitchen to outside cabins while the woman smiles.

Frank
See baby I just wanted us to have a great time.

EXT. Cabin

While Frank was dragging Carrie across the dirt outside going back toward their cabins. Carrie starts to open her eyes slowly while Frank opens the front door of their cabin. Frank drags Carrie on the side of the sofa he drops her legs and he started to run upstairs. So, Carrie looks to the right in she sees a door was crack a door that she never seen sense she been at the cabin. so, she gets up off the floor to walk toward the door She opens the door it smells like a basement Carrie turns the lights on in the basement.

Frank started to run down the stairs and he didn't see Carrie nowhere.

Lights flashing on and off.

INT. Cabin basement cellur.

Frank
Where are you?

Frank walks toward the kitchen and he see a door open.so he walked toward the door while Carrie was looking around the basement and she sees two gas cans.

Sitting on a shelf. Carrie started to grab the cans off the shelf to pour the gas over the basement. So, Frank started to walk down the stairs Carrie hides under the stairs.

Frank
I smell gas Carrie what you been doing?

Frank looks around didn't see Carrie frank walks a little close to the back Carrie come out from under the stairs.

Carrie
Baby I love you. But you Must die again in this place.

Frank
What is you talking about I'm here?

Carrie walks backwards slowly a tear started to run down her left eye. She reaches in her pocket to grab a lighter.

Carrie
I'm sorry frank burn in hell you broke my heart.

Carrie drops the lighter immediately fire flames started to appear all over the basement burning Frank while Carrie run back upstairs to run outside.

Frank
No!!

EXT. OUTSIDE CABIN-DAWN

Camera fades out creature was burning by the old abandon cabin in the woods.

Camera fade in by Carrie

Cabins burning around Carrie she drops to her kneels and started to cry.

Carrie (cry's)
So, well frank

Camera slowly fade away black smoke going up into the sky's fire burning.

END CREDITS.

Printed in the United States
By Bookmasters